J F BOD

Body, Wendy.

Mup's days of the week

MUP'S
Days of the Week

Published in the United States by
QEB Publishing, Inc.
23062 La Cadena Drive
Laguna Hills, CA 92653
www.qeb-publishing.com

Library of Congress Control Number 2005921268

ISBN 1-59566-104-2

Written by Wendy Body
Designed by Alix Wood
Editor Hannah Ray
Illustrated by Sanja Rescek

Series Consultant Anne Faundez
Publisher Steve Evans
Creative Director Louise Morley
Editorial Manager Jean Coppendale

Printed and bound in China

QEB WordBanks

Learning Words with Monsters

MUP'S

Days of the Week

Wendy Body

QEB Publishing, Inc.

On **Monday**, Mup climbed a mountain with a rainbow in his pocket.

Monday

Tuesday

Wednesday

Thursday

Friday

Saturday

Sunday

627536

On **Tuesday**, he flew to the
moon and back in a shiny,
silver rocket.

Monday

Tuesday

Wednesday

Thursday

Friday

Saturday

Sunday

On **Wednesday**, he walked to the North Pole and played with a polar bear.

Monday

Tuesday

Wednesday

Thursday

Friday

Saturday

Sunday

On **Thursday**, he made an enormous cake for all his friends to share.

Monday

Tuesday

Wednesday

Thursday

Friday

Saturday

Sunday

On **Friday**, he had a ride on a whale and went sailing all over the sea.

Monday

Tuesday

Wednesday

Thursday

Friday

Saturday

Sunday

On **Saturday**, he built a castle at the top of a very tall tree.

Monday

Tuesday

Wednesday

Thursday

Friday

Saturday

Sunday

On **Sunday**, he went in
a hot-air balloon to fly all
over the sky, and painted
the clouds with purple
paint when they came
drifting by.

Monday

Tuesday

Wednesday

Thursday

Friday

Saturday

Sunday

Mup's calendar

Monday

climbed a mountain

Tuesday

flew to the moon

Wednesday

walked to the
North Pole

Thursday
made an enormous
cake

Friday
rode on a whale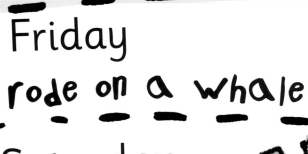

Saturday

built a castle

Sunday

painted the clouds

Things to do

Can you complete the sentences by pointing to the right day of the week?

Monday
Saturday
Wednesday
Friday
Thursday
Sunday
Tuesday

On _____ Mup climbed a mountain.
On _____ Mup flew to the moon.
On _____ Mup walked to the North Pole.
On _____ Mup made an enormous cake.
On _____ Mup rode on a whale.
On _____ Mup built a castle.
On _____ Mup painted the clouds.

Things to do

Can you remember how the words for these pictures begin?

Which words begin with the same sound?

Word bank

Words from the story

balloon
bear
cake
castle
cloud
moon
mountain
pocket
rainbow
rocket
sea
tree
whale

Action words

built
climbed
flew
painted
played
walked

Word bank

Words and endings

		More action words
build	built	draw
climb	climbed	hop
fly	flew	jump
paint	painted	run
play	played	skip
walk	walked	sit
		swim
What do you notice		stand
about these words?		

Parents' and teachers' notes

- As you read the book to your child, run your finger underneath the text. This will help your child follow the reading and focus on how the words look, as well as how they sound.

- Once your child is familiar with the book, encourage him or her to join in with the reading—especially the days of the week.

- Help your child to see and understand the illustrations. Use open-ended questions to encourage him or her to respond; for example, "What's happening on this page?" "What is Mup doing here?" "Could he really do that?"

- Practice saying the days of the week in order.

- Can your child remember what Mup did on each specific day?

- Encourage your child to express opinions and preferences. Ask questions such as: "Which picture do you like most? Why?" "Which part of the book did you like best?" "Which day do you think Mup enjoyed most?" "If you could do any of the things that Mup did, which would you choose? Why?"

- Ask your child to make comparisons between Mup and himself or herself; for example, "Today is Monday. What did Mup do yesterday? What did you do yesterday?" Discuss what your child does over the course of a week. Are there certain activities he or she does on specific days?

- Talk about Mup and discuss the monster's appearance. Encourage your child to invent and describe a monster of his or her own. What would the monster like to do? What would feature in the monster's calendar?

- Draw your child's attention to the structure of some words—especially the days of the week. Look at how each one includes the smaller word "day." Explain that this can help us to remember how the words are spelled; "Wednesday" is spelled "Wed–nes–day."

- Read the instructions/questions on the "Things to do" pages (pages 20–21) to your child and help him or her with the answers where necessary. Give your child lots of encouragement and praise. Even if he or she gets something wrong you can say, "That was a really good try, but it's not that one, it's this one."

- Read and discuss the words on the "Word bank" pages (pages 22–23). Look at the letter patterns together and how the words are spelled. Cover up the first part of a word and see if your child can remember what was there. See if your child can write the easier words from memory—he or she will probably need several attempts to write a word correctly!

- When you are talking about letter sounds, try not to add too much of an uh or er sound. Say mmm instead of muh or mer, ssss instead of suh or ser. Saying letter sounds as carefully as possible will help your child when he or she is trying to build up or spell words—tah-o-pa doesn't sound much like "top"!

- Talk about words: what they mean, how they sound, how they look, and how they are spelled. However, if your child gets restless or bored, stop. Enjoyment of the story, activity, or book is essential if children are going to grow up valuing books and reading!